Puppy on the Farm

By Marilyn Elson
Illustrated by Lisa McCue

previously titled *Duffy on the Farm*

A GOLDEN BOOK • NEW YORK
Western Publishing Company, Inc., Racine, Wisconsin 53404

 ISBN: 0-307-00333-7
MCMXC

Once there was a frisky puppy named Duffy. He lived with his mother and brothers and sister down the road from Mr. Potter's farm.

Duffy thought he could find some new friends on the farm. So one morning he wandered off to see it—all by himself.

Duffy went inside the barn. Suddenly he heard a strange low noise.

Moo-o-o-o-o! It was a cow.

The cow was very big, so the puppy hopped onto the milking stool. “Hello,” said Duffy. “Will you play with me?”

“Moo-o-o-o-o!” said the cow again. “I’m too busy munching on hay.”

So Duffy scampered off.

Outside the barn, Duffy saw a kitten. She was asleep in the straw.

“Arf! Arf! Arf!” said Duffy. “Let’s play hide-and-seek.”

Duffy's loud barking woke the kitten up.
"Meow, meow," she said. "I can't play with you. I'm taking my nap."

So Duffy hurried on.

A plump piglet was wading in a puddle.

"Can I play with you in that puddle?" asked Duffy.

"Oink, oink, oink!" said the piglet. "This puddle is too small for a piglet *and* a puppy!" He sent Duffy away with a SPLASH!

The hungry cow, the sleepy kitten, and the plump piglet would not play with Duffy. But that frisky puppy still wanted to find a friend on the farm. So on he went.

Duffy came to the chicken coop. A mother hen and her fuzzy yellow chicks were eating grain.

"Hello," said Duffy. "Let's all play follow-the-leader."

But the mother hen said, “Cluck! Cluck! I can’t play with you. I must stay here with my babies.”

The seven fuzzy chicks said, “Cheep, cheep, cheep! There’s lots more grain to eat. Cheep, cheep, cheep!”

So Duffy went on his way.

Duffy came to a field where he saw a horse out grazing.

He jumped up to the fence and said, "I've met the cow, the kitten, the piglet, the hen, and the chicks. But they won't play with me. Will you?"

"Neigh-h-h-h-h!" said the horse. "You'd better hurry home. Don't you know it's suppertime?"

How lonely Duffy felt. He looked out at the field. Then he looked back at the barn. "Which way is home?" he wondered. "Now I am lost, and hungry, too."

Arf! Arf! Arf! Duffy knew *that* sound. It was Mother! He raced to meet her.

Mother and the other puppies were coming down the road toward Mr. Potter's farm.

“There you are,” said Mother. “We’ve finally found you!”

"We're hungry for our supper!" said Duffy's brothers and his sister. "Let's go home right now."

"I'm hungry, too," said Duffy. "And after supper we can play hide-and-seek and follow-the-leader and lots of other games."

"Arf! Arf! Arf! Arf!" said the happy puppies all at once. They were together at last.

“Home is the best place for me!” said Duffy.